THE VIOLIN MAN

Maureen Brett Hooper

Illustrations by
Gary Undercuffler

CAROLINE HOUSE

Published by Caroline House
Boyds Mills Press, Inc.
A Highlights Company
910 Church Street
Honesdale, Pennsylvania 18431

Publisher-Cataloging-in-Publication Data
Hooper, Maureen Brett
    The Violin Man/by Maureen Brett Hooper
    78 p.: ill.; cm.
Summary: A nineteenth-century story of the search for a lost
Stradivarius violin. The events of the search make exciting
adventure.
ISBN 1-878093-79-7
1. Violins—Fiction—Juvenile literature. [1. Violins—Fiction.]
I. Title.
[F]   1991
LC Card number 91-70417

First edition, 1991
Book designed by Charlotte Staub
Distributed by St. Martin's Press
Printed in the United States of America

To Jeffrey, a special young friend

AUTHOR'S NOTE

Luigi Tarisio was a real person who traveled through the villages and towns of Italy in the 1880s searching for lost Stradivarius violins.

While the details of this story have been created from my imagination, I am certain that such events would have happened to Luigi in his travels if he had been lucky enough to meet someone like Antonio.

CHAPTER
1

The Traveling Man

Antonio ate as fast as he could, keeping one eye on his food and the other on the door.

"What have you been doing all morning?" his father's voice boomed at him from the end of the table.

And Antonio knew he had no chance to escape.

"Nothing, Papa," he muttered, jamming a spoon full of food into his mouth.

His brothers and sisters giggled. They knew, as well as he, what always came next.

"Have you been daydreaming again?"

"No, Papa."

His father shook his fork at Antonio. "No daydreaming—do you hear?"

Antonio's face flushed. "I wasn't daydreaming, Papa!" he answered. "All morning I've watched a traveling man coming down the valley. He's climbing the hill right now and . . ." Antonio shuddered as a thundercloud crossed his father's face.

"Traveling man!" His father was shouting now. "Is that all you ever think about?"

Antonio yelled back. (At least, he yelled as loud as he dared.) "But I'm going to be a traveling man someday."

His father growled. And Antonio was sure he would explode any minute.

Just in time his mother helped. "Give the boy a chance, Papa."

With a shrug, his father went back to eating.

Antonio stole a look to the end of the table and wondered why his father never understood.

At ten, although he wished otherwise, Antonio thought of himself as just ordinary. He looked pretty much like everyone he knew. He was an ordinary shape. He was an ordinary size. And, as with all his friends, he had ordinary feet that rarely saw the insides of shoes.

He lived in an ordinary town. One that was very much like so many others in Italy, huddled against a hill, surrounded by vineyards and topped by a monastery.

It was only when traveling men came to town that Antonio got ideas about a life that could be anything but ordinary. When he was lucky the men would come down the valley and climb up to his town.

When he was luckier still he would meet them and ask them all sorts of questions.

Antonio had heard at least a hundred stories from traveling men. There were stories about boats, about trains, and all sorts of things. Some stories were so strange that even Antonio had trouble believing them.

Once a traveling man, seeing that Antonio doubted him, had said, "*E'vero*, it is true, Antonio, what I tell you. We're living in the 1800s. Important things are happening out there."

Although he had never even been down to the valley, Antonio believed the man. One day he would go and see for himself.

Now Antonio scraped the last bites of food from his plate and thought about the traveling man coming up his hill that very minute.

He refused his favorite pudding. His mother shook her head and swept him from the table. He shot for the door—not giving his father the chance to stop him.

The sun told him he had better hurry or he wouldn't get to the edge of town in time to meet the traveling man. He made a lucky wish up to the monastery and rushed down the narrow street. His bare feet navigated the slippery cobblestones. His whole body worked against the steepness of the hill.

He passed the fruit shop without taking a single glance into the boxes lined up out front. He didn't pause at the baker's shop, either, in spite of the delicious odor of warm sweet buns.

It wasn't until he reached the shoemaker's shop that he hesitated even a little bit. He knew he had to be careful. That horrible little man was always catching hold of him to ask a thousand questions. "I am the mayor, you know," he would say, as if that made it a law.

Taking a deep breath, Antonio scurried by. But not without seeing a beady pair of eyes glaring out at him.

He raced by the butcher shop. Its small sign advertising *Franco Meats* swung gently in the breeze above the door. Out of habit, he edged to the other side of the street.

As he approached Papa Parducci's candle shop he thought he saw the white lace curtain in the window flutter a bit. He put his eyes down and kept moving.

In another minute he reached the edge of town. He left the cobblestones behind for the dust of the winding road. He rounded the first bend sure he would find the traveling man. The road was empty. He had no better luck around the second bend, or the third.

Antonio began to run, his legs and arms going in all directions. He was reaching his greatest speed as he turned around yet another bend and crashed into something. He flew into the air and landed on his back. He looked up to see what he had hit. It was the traveling man!

"What is this that tried to knock me over?" the man said. "Is it a falling rock? A battering ram?" A grin covered the man's face. "No," he added, "it's a young man." He pulled Antonio to his feet. "Hello there. I'm Luigi."

"I'm Antonio." Antonio looked from Luigi to his bulking pack and back again.

"Where do you come from?" he asked.

Antonio didn't wait for an answer. "How long will you stay? Have you been on a train? A boat?"

He ran around to have a better look at the man's pack. "What are you selling?" he said. When he noticed a shallow, rectangular box hanging from the pack, he pointed and said, "What's that?"

Without a word, Luigi adjusted his pack and

started up the hill again. Antonio followed.

It wasn't until they had gone some distance that the traveling man began to talk. "I'm from Milan, a city to the north. I won't stay long."

He nodded his head in Antonio's direction. "Yes, I've been on a train. And a boat, too."

He studied the road, as if forgetting what came next. "Oh, yes, I've nothing to sell."

"What then?" Antonio insisted. His eyes surveyed the pack on Luigi's back again, looking for new clues.

"I've come to find something."

"Find something?" Antonio repeated. "What?"

"A treasure."

Antonio's voice was flat with suspicion. "A treasure? In this town?"

Luigi didn't answer. He pointed up the hill and shifted his pack. "I need to get into town and find a place for the night."

And Antonio knew he wouldn't get any more answers, at least not right then.

Luigi reached back and untied the small box. "Here," he said. "If you like, you can help make my load a little lighter."

Antonio took the box. It wasn't heavy. He wondered what could be in a box that shape and size. Should he ask?

But one look at Luigi's face, set against the strain of the climb, made him wait. Without another word, Antonio and Luigi walked into town.

CHAPTER
2

The Box

Antonio looked neither to the left nor the right as they walked up the street. He lifted the box into plain sight and worked to make it look larger and heavier than it really was. He held his head high, as if to say, "Look at me. I'm with a traveling man."

Some people stopped to stare. The small sign advertising *Franco Meats* still swung gently in the breeze above the door to the butcher shop. The curtain in the candle shop window definitely fluttered a bit. Once again Antonio was sure he saw the shoemaker's beady eyes peering out of his shop.

They had nearly reached the top of the town when Antonio pointed out his house. It stood firmly squeezed between its neighbors, a handsome house of yellow stucco and red tile. A small tree had somehow found room to grow near the door. It was the only tree in the whole town.

"Wait here, under my tree," Antonio said. "Wait here, and I'll see if you can stay the night." He disappeared inside.

Luigi had barely put his pack down and leaned against the tree before Antonio was back.

"You can stay," he shouted and motioned to Luigi. "If you don't mind the shed."

Antonio helped Luigi move in. The shed was a storeroom. It was built against the back of the house. It wasn't very grand, but Luigi seemed pleased.

Antonio watched Luigi pull his belongings from his pack. First there was a bedroll. Together they worked to move barrels and sacks to make room for it on the earthen floor. Next came Luigi's clothes. The traveling man folded them and placed them high on an empty shelf.

They made a table by putting several boards across two barrels. On the makeshift table, Luigi set out the strangest assortment of things Antonio had ever seen. There was a good-sized magnifying glass, a knife with a long narrow blade, a giant pair of pliers that looked like those the barber used to pull teeth. There was a peculiar metal hook and at least a half dozen pairs of wooden clamps.

Antonio was even more puzzled when Luigi pulled from his pack a pot of glue and a tiny stove. But he followed Luigi's instructions and put them on the floor next to the table.

Antonio's questions flew around the shed. "What is this? What is that? How does this work? How does that work? What will you do with this? What will you do with that?"

But Luigi ignored them all.

When the box was put in a corner, leaning against the wall, Luigi gently pushed Antonio out the door with the promise, "We'll talk soon."

But it didn't seem soon at all. Antonio had to wait the rest of the afternoon. And all through supper, too.

At supper time Antonio's father did most of the talking. "So you're a traveling man, are you?" he said to Luigi, who sat at the other end of the table.

"I am," Luigi said. He looked Antonio's father straight in the eye.

"My son seems to think there's something good about being a traveling man."

"It has its good points. And its bad," Luigi replied.

Antonio opened his mouth to say something, then decided he'd better not.

Antonio's father glared out at the traveling man. "Don't you ever want to stay in one place?"

"Someday. But for now I have something important to do. It keeps me traveling."

"Urumph, what can be so important?" Antonio's father muttered. He went back to scraping at the food on his plate.

Antonio's mother spoke. "We would miss our son if he ever went away." There was a mist in her eyes.

Luigi smiled at her. "They say if you love someone you will set him free."

No more was said.

They finished supper. Without a word, Antonio's father left the table. Antonio's mother sent his brothers and sisters off to bed and made herself busy with the dishes.

Antonio knew it was his turn at last.

He edged up to Luigi. "The treasure," he whispered, "does it have anything to do with the box?"

Luigi's face lighted up. "Why don't you go and get it. We'll open it. You can see for yourself."

In seconds Antonio was back. He held the box out to Luigi.

Luigi shook his head. "You open it."

Antonio put it on the floor next to Luigi's chair and knelt before it. He studied it and found the clasp that held it closed. Releasing the lock, he raised the lid.

Antonio looked into the box and then quickly up to Luigi. "It's empty," he said. "It's empty."

He couldn't believe it. Except for a lining of blue velvet, the box was absolutely empty—like a tiny coffin.

Had he done all this waiting for an empty box?

Luigi held his hands out to match the measurements of the box and in a teasing voice said, "The treasure I came looking for . . . well . . . it will be just that size."

Antonio's mind raced. What could fill that space? He searched Luigi's face for more clues. None came. "What goes in the box?" he demanded.

"Why Antonio," Luigi answered as if he thought Antonio should already know. "A violin, of course."

Antonio's whole body slumped. Not if he had thought forever would he have guessed a violin. "I thought gold, maybe, or jewels." His voice was choked with disappointment.

"Oh, but the violin I'm looking for might be worth more than a box of gold," Luigi said.

Antonio didn't believe him for a minute. He had seen a violin. "A violin can't be worth much," he said.

Luigi motioned Antonio to sit next to him. "Let me tell you about this violin."

Antonio slid into the chair. The lamp in the center of the table gave off a circle of light that seemed to close out everything but Luigi's face. In seconds Antonio was settled and ready to listen.

"This violin is old, very old," Luigi began. "Perhaps it was made as long as one hundred years ago."

"A hundred years old!" Antonio cried out. His grandfather had built their house fifty years ago. Antonio thought that was about as old as anything could be, except maybe the monastery.

But still, Luigi's treasure was just a violin, and who cared about a violin! Antonio made a face.

Luigi laughed at the look. "It's not just any violin, Antonio. It's a Stradivarius. A violin made by Antonio Stradivari."

Even Antonio had to smile at hearing his own name. "But . . ."

Luigi didn't wait. "Antonio Stradivari had his violin shop in Cremona. Have you heard of that town?"

Antonio shook his head.

"No matter." And Luigi went on. "People came to Cremona from all over to buy Stradivarius violins. Many said Stradivari made the best violins in the country. Some said they were the best in the whole world."

For a minute Luigi was lost in his thoughts. "His violins are wonderful to see and hear," he murmured. "But most of all, I guess, they are wonderful to play."

Antonio squirmed and waited for Luigi to go on. "I understand," he said. "Anyway, I think I do. But still . . . a treasure . . . that's usually something more important than . . . I don't know . . ." And his voice trailed off to nothing.

Luigi smiled at Antonio. "Even today a violinist will pay almost anything to own one." He pursed his lips and looked very serious. "That is, when and if I find one."

"Are you good at it—finding violins?"

"Usually. Some call me the Violin Man."

"The Violin Man!"

Antonio cradled his chin in his hands and stared at Luigi for a long time. Finally, he spoke. "If you find one here in town, will that be important?"

Luigi nodded.

"Not just something ordinary?" Antonio whispered.

"I would think it would be anything but that."

And, in the smallest voice yet, Antonio asked, "Could I help?"

Luigi, without the slightest hesitation, answered, "That would be fine."

Antonio shot from his chair like a cannon ball. "Where do we start?" he shouted.

Luigi laughed. "I'll show you the diary in the morning."

"Diary?"

"In the morning," Luigi repeated.

CHAPTER
3

The Diary

When Antonio woke up he didn't have an idea what time it was. Up under the eaves where he slept it was always dark.

He sat up, almost hitting his head. It was a special day, he knew that much. But for a minute he couldn't remember why. Then it came back— the Violin Man!

He jumped out of bed, grabbed his clothes, and headed for the stairs, hoping he wasn't too late. He went down the steps two at a time, doing a balancing act as he dressed.

He relaxed when he found Luigi at the table.

"You didn't forget did you?" Antonio asked.

Luigi shook his head. "I've been waiting for you."

Antonio's mother, standing near the stove, turned and pointed to the table. "First, you sit and eat, Antonio. Whatever you two are planning can wait." Between swallows Antonio found time to ask Luigi about the diary.

Luigi pulled a small book with a leather cover from his coat pocket. "I picked up this diary in a little antique odds-and-ends shop in Milan," he said. "It led me to your town."

He opened the book where a blue ribbon marked the page. He read aloud: *"Today, again, I heard the magic violin. It grows more beautiful each time."*

Antonio's eyes grew wide. With a giant gulp he emptied his bowl, pushed it away, and asked, "But why here . . . in this town?"

The Violin Man turned to the inside cover. "Look."

Antonio stretched his neck for a better view. In one corner, in neat old-fashioned script, was the town's name. For the first time Antonio really believed there might be a violin in town.

He looked again. Under the town's name was a date that showed the diary was very old.

And when he reached the bottom of the page he saw the words: *Into this diary go all the happenings of my life.* A signature was scrawled beneath it.

Carefully, Antonio's fingers traced the signature. He knew it was important to the clue. "Angelina," he read, his voice cracking. But when he tried to read the last name, his hope for finding the violin drained away. No matter how hard he worked at it he couldn't make it out.

"It's not much, is it?" Luigi said as if reading Antonio's mind. "But don't give up. We have a chance. We just have to find this Angelina's family name, that's all."

That's *all*, Antonio thought. That's impossible, he wanted to shout. And he was about to tell Luigi so when *I am the mayor*, popped into his head. If anyone could help them it would be the mayor. Any man who asked that many questions had to know everything.

Antonio was almost out the door and headed for the shoemaker's shop before he remembered Luigi. "Come on," he shouted over his shoulder. "The mayor . . . he'll know."

They found the mayor in front of his shop. The little man grabbed at Antonio. His beady eyes glared. His rancid breath reached Antonio's nose. "Well, boy, you finally decided to bring your friend to see me. It's about time, too, boy. Thought I didn't see you yesterday, did you?"

Abruptly the mayor pushed Antonio away and poked his finger in Luigi's direction. "And you, who are you? Why are you in my town? I am the mayor, you know."

Antonio didn't wait for Luigi. "This is Luigi, Mr. Mayor. He's here to find a treasure." Antonio knew from the look on the mayor's face he had said the wrong thing.

"A treasure!" the mayor shouted and waved his arms in the air. "You've come to steal from us? I won't have it. Do you understand?"

Antonio tried again. "He isn't going to steal

anything, Mr. Mayor. He just wants to take it back to Milan." In an instant he knew that was no better.

"Milan! Milan!" The mayor was screaming now and marching up and down. "We can't have big city people coming here and taking things from our town."

Antonio tried once more. "It would be an honor for our town." Seeing he had the mayor's attention, he quickly added, "And for the mayor, too."

"An honor, you say?" The mayor calmed down and took a new look at the Violin Man. "Well, sir, welcome to my town." He bowed. "I am the mayor, you know."

"Yes, Mr. Mayor, indeed I do."

"Now." The mayor rubbed his hands together as if matters were settled. "Tell me what I can do for you?"

Antonio told the story—all about the violin and the old diary; about the name Angelina and the missing last name.

When Antonio finished, the mayor invited them inside.

The shop was filled with the odor of shoe leather and polish. At one side was the shoemaker's bench surrounded by piles of shoes and boots in all states of repair.

But the mayor didn't stop. He motioned them to the side of the shop where the office of the mayor was located. A black robe hung from a rack. A red ribbon with an official looking medal at its end hung beside it. On a desk were piles of ledgers and all sorts of official documents.

"The mayor is responsible for the town's records, you know," the mayor boasted. "That's why I ask so many questions."

He pointed to his desk as if he were proud of the jumble. "You say about one hundred years ago, do you?" And the mayor pulled a book from the pile.

"Well . . . well this is difficult . . . definitely difficult," he said with his head buried in the ledger. "But I can do it. I can definitely do it."

And he did. He found the right place in his book and the names of *two* Angelinas. He grinned. "About that time there was Angelina Franco and Angelina Parducci. Take your pick!"

The mayor was puffed with pride as Luigi and Antonio left the shop. He waved after them, calling out, "I am the mayor, you know."

Antonio couldn't believe their luck. He was so excited he could hardly get the words out. "We have a Franco . . . and a Parducci . . . living here . . . living right here . . . right now."

"Tell me about them," Luigi said.

Antonio calmed himself a bit. "Mr. Franco is the butcher. His shop is just down there." Antonio pointed to where the small sign advertising *Franco Meats* swung gently in the breeze above the door. "Papa Parducci lives over there. He's the candlestick maker." He pointed across the street to the shop with the white lace curtain.

"Which one should we visit first?" Luigi asked.

Mr. Franco was the largest and loudest man Antonio had ever known. Antonio avoided him whenever possible. Although he never admitted it, he was just a little afraid of the butcher and his giant-sized knives.

On the other hand, Papa Parducci was the oldest man he'd ever known. He couldn't remember things very well. Although Antonio tried, he had a hard time being patient with him.

Antonio weighed the good and the bad about each man and made up his mind. "Papa Parducci," he said. "Let's go see him."

CHAPTER

4

The Search

The jingle of the bell above the door echoed through the shop as Antonio pushed his way inside. Luigi followed. In the dimness of the shop, the shadowy fingers of long slender candles, hanging about on racks, gave a ghostly feeling.

Antonio searched the shop until he found Papa Parducci in a far corner. The old man was slumped in a rocking chair fast asleep. His chin rested on his chest and his mouth hung slack. Even as he slept, his hands held tightly to his cane.

"Eh? Eh?" Papa Parducci said as he woke up. He peered out into the shop. "Who's there?" he called. His voice was high and raspy.

"It's me, Papa Parducci," Antonio said.

"Who?" The man peered down his nose through the tiny spectacles resting precariously at its tip.

"It's me—Antonio."

"I knew that. Just give me a little time to think."

The old man pointed his cane toward the Violin Man. "And who are you? Don't know you. What do you want?"

Luigi shouted, "I'm Luigi, Mr. Parducci!"

"Don't shout. I can hear you, young man."

He pointed to Antonio and said, "Did you tell him I was deaf? Well, I'm not. Hear just fine, thank you. Well, now you're here, tell me what you want."

Antonio planted his feet firmly before the old man and told his story just as he had for the mayor. Only this time he added the information about the names in the town ledger. He finished with, "Do you have the violin?"

"Come closer, so I can see you. What did you say your name was?"

And Antonio knew right then that Papa Parducci had not understood one thing he had said. He didn't mean to but he shouted at the old man. "I'm ANTONIO. He's LUIGI. We're hunting for a VIOLIN. Do you know an ANGELINA?"

Papa Parducci stared at the ceiling. A tear ran down his cheek. "Angelina?" he muttered. "That was my mother's name."

"Papa Parducci." Antonio moved closer and coaxed the old man. "Where's the violin? You must have it somewhere."

"Have what? What do you want?"

Why can't the old man remember anything, Antonio thought. Why can't he remember—just this once?

Papa Parducci looked back and forth at Antonio and Luigi. "What are you looking for? I have candles, lots and lots of candles."

By the time Antonio and Luigi left the shop, Papa Parducci was sound asleep again, his hands holding tightly to his cane.

Antonio stared at the sign in front of the butcher shop. He gathered his courage and led the Violin Man inside.

They stopped at the door to let their eyes grow accustomed to the dim light. Huge shanks of meat hung from giant hooks; strings of sausages decorated the rafters; ducks and chickens, swinging by their necks, filled the window.

"Good morning," a voice boomed from the back of

the shop. Mr. Franco stood there patting his over-stuffed stomach and grinning at them.

Everything about the butcher was large. His chest was as big as a pickle barrel, and his arms as large as the ham shanks he sold. His hands were colossal, his feet super colossal; even his nose was a good size.

"Ah, Antonio, it's you," the butcher said. "What can I give you today? Does your mother want maybe something special for supper?"

"Good morning, Mr. Franco," Antonio replied. There was a little shake in his voice. "This is Luigi. He came down the valley yesterday. He's looking for something. . . ." That was as far as Antonio could go. His tongue seemed to swell and his mouth went dry.

The butcher wiped his hand on his apron and held it out to Luigi. "What can I do for you, Mr. Luigi? Are you looking maybe for sausages? I have special kinds. I make them myself."

Before the butcher could reach for the sausages, Luigi answered, "No thank you, Mr. Franco. I've not come for your sausages."

Mr. Franco looked puzzled. "If not my sausages, what then?" He leaned across the large chopping block and placed his hands dangerously near his knives.

Antonio pulled in his breath and took several steps back—just behind Luigi.

Luigi told the story, all about the diary and the violin.

"It's a Stradivarius," Antonio added, poking his head out just long enough to say the words.

When Luigi mentioned the name Angelina, Mr.

Franco nodded. "Ah, yes," he said. "That was the name of my uncle's wife. Before that, I don't know."

Antonio poked his head out again. "Do you have the violin?"

The butcher thought for a minute. "I have a violin. I play it sometimes for town dances. But it's nothing special. You know, Antonio."

Antonio agreed. "Not that violin. This one will have a beautiful sound." In his excitement, he stepped out in full sight.

The butcher threw back his head and let out a belly laugh so loud that Antonio immediately went back into hiding.

"Well, no one says my playing is beautiful," Mr. Franco said.

"I know," Antonio said. And he inched his way toward the door, ready to run.

But Mr. Franco only held up his fingers the size and shape of his sausages. "Don't blame the violin. These are not the hands of a great fiddle player." And with that he let out such a roar that Antonio had to hold his hands over his ears.

"What do you say? Maybe I play for you?" the butcher suggested. Without another word, he brought out his violin. He held it against his chest (there was no way he could get it under his chin where it belonged), grabbed roughly at the bow, and began to play. It was a rollicking tune. And, considering the size of his hands and the width of his fingers, the butcher played it well. It was true the violin did not sound beautiful, but soon both Antonio and Luigi were tapping their toes and smiling. Antonio even came out in plain sight.

When the butcher finished, Luigi carried the violin to the shop window. He pushed aside the chickens and the ducks hanging by their necks and held the violin to the light. Turning it over and over in his hands, he examined every inch.

Antonio crowded in close, trying to find out what Luigi was seeing. Luigi stood there so long that Antonio began to think they had found the right violin. "Is it a Stradivarius?" he asked, trying to keep the excitement out of his voice.

"It's difficult to say, but . . ." Luigi left the sentence dangling. He held the violin up to the window again. "If it's a Stradivarius it will say so on the label. The label should be just about here." He squinted through one of the carved holes. "Just about here," he repeated.

"What does it say?" In his eagerness, Antonio almost knocked Luigi over.

Luigi lowered the violin and turned from the window. The shop was silent. Slowly Luigi put his free hand on Antonio's shoulder. To Antonio it felt like a hundred-pound weight.

When at last the Violin Man spoke, his voice was just as heavy. "This is not our Stradivarius, Antonio."

And Antonio felt ordinary again.

CHAPTER
5

The Rim of the World

Antonio couldn't eat his noon meal. The lump in his throat made it hard to swallow.

He pushed his food around the plate, only half listening to his father and Luigi talk.

"So you have been out in the town this morning," Antonio's father began. He poked his fork in Luigi's direction.

"I have," Luigi replied.

"Something about a violin, I hear. That's how you spend your time? Looking for violins?" Antonio's father shook his head in disbelief.

"From the time I was very young I knew that was to be my life," Luigi said. He pressed forward in his chair. "They are not just any violins. They are masterpieces."

"I see," Antonio's father said. Still, he shook his head.

Luigi went on. "If I don't find them, they will remain lost and forgotten. And that would not be good." He waved his hands in the air. "Don't you see? These violins must be played again. People must hear them."

Antonio's father said nothing. He looked from Luigi to Antonio and back again. A puzzled look crossed his face.

"And Antonio is helping you?" he asked. There was a new softness in his eyes.

Luigi nodded. "He is."

"I see," his father said. "Well, Antonio, did you find this violin your traveling man talks of?"

Antonio didn't look up from his plate. "No, Papa," he whispered. His stomach twisted and turned.

No more was said.

As soon as he could, Antonio got up from the table and left the house. He walked, hardly noticing where he was going. He wound up on the road to the valley. Yesterday it had been exciting there. Today it was no fun at all.

Partway down he came to a giant boulder. It jutted out over the side of the hill like a large blemish on the landscape. He scrambled to the top and sat there, hanging on the rim of the world. That was just fine with him. He wanted to be far away from everything and everyone.

He scooped up a loose pebble and threw it. Seconds later he heard it fall somewhere out of sight.

Not finding the violin had been the mayor's fault, he thought. That little man boasted about being so important. He probably didn't know nearly as much as he pretended.

And it was Papa Parducci's fault. That old man couldn't remember a thing.

It was Mr. Franco's fault, too. He was all noise and bluff.

Antonio picked up another stone and gave it a great heave. His thoughts raced. It was the town's fault. It's just a dull, terrible town. And Luigi's fault. Why had he come to town anyway? And the violin's fault. Why had it been made? Or lost? Or . . . or? . . .

Antonio picked up another stone. This time he didn't throw it. He turned it over in his hand, examining every chip and crack.

He knew what was really wrong.

Luigi was probably packing to leave this very minute. And it was all Antonio's fault.

This time he threw his stone so far he was sure it would never fall to the ground. Not even being on the rim of the world helped anymore. He climbed down and started back to town.

On his way he tried to catch a lizard. But it ran ahead of him and dashed under a rock just in time. I can't do anything right, he thought.

He found the Violin Man standing under the tree. Luigi was busy watching the smoke from his afternoon pipe trail up and out on the breeze.

Antonio stood beside him waiting to be noticed.

When the Violin Man finally looked down, he seemed surprised. "Ah, there you are, *amico mio*, my friend. Have you been standing there long? Come, let's talk."

In the shed they sat on two barrels in front of the makeshift table. Luigi tapped his fingers on the boards to some tune he seemed to be hearing in his head. Antonio inhaled the special odors of the shed. In the warmth of the afternoon, the aroma of the grain and potatoes filled the room.

Antonio looked at the strange assortment of things the Violin Man had placed on the table. He still didn't know what they were or why Luigi carried them. And maybe now he would never know.

Finally Antonio and Luigi faced each other and began to talk.

At first neither of them mentioned the violin. They talked, instead, about trains and boats, cities and buildings.

Then the conversation dwindled to nothing and they had to talk about the violin.

"I'm sorry, Luigi," Antonio began. "It was my fault we didn't find the violin." The words hurt. Antonio couldn't make himself look at the Violin Man.

"No, Antonio. It was nobody's fault," Luigi replied. "It is often difficult to find something that has been missing for so long."

His hand fell on Antonio's shoulder. "Now what should we do next?" he asked.

"You're not going to leave?" Antonio shouted. "I thought . . ." His eyes opened wide.

"Do you want to give up?" Luigi teased.

"Oh, no!"

"I have a feeling the violin is here somewhere. If only . . ."

Antonio jumped up. "I could find a new clue," he offered.

"That would help."

Antonio looked over the table and found the little diary with its leather cover. He reached for it. "I'll take the diary," he said. "And just maybe . . ."

Later, sitting under his tree, Antonio opened the little book to the page marked with the blue ribbon. *Today, again, I heard the magic violin*, he read. *It grows more beautiful each time*. He stared at the words and worked to find his new clue.

What had he missed?

At school, his teacher had told him to look at both sides. It was worth a try. Looking at the diary, he asked: What does it say? And what does it *not* say?

He listed all of the important words: today, I, heard, magic, violin, beautiful, each, time.

What the diary didn't say was much harder to see. "Well," he said out loud, "it doesn't say Franco or Parducci."

Then he was stuck.

He forced himself to go on. His whole body ached from the effort. "It doesn't say . . . my, mine, played." Just then he felt something happen. Somehow he knew if he reached out and took hold he would have the right clue. But it was like grabbing for water.

In the next instant the answer came. "The violin

didn't belong to Angelina or her family." The words came out of his mouth from deep inside. "Angelina only *heard* the magic violin."

And Antonio knew. He had not asked Mr. Franco or Papa Parducci the right question.

CHAPTER
6

The New
Question

It was early the next morning when Antonio reached Mr. Franco's shop. The butcher had not arrived yet. Antonio waited outside, rehearsing what he had to say. He hoped this time his tongue would not get stuck.

The new question ran through his head. If he were lucky, he would find a new clue for Luigi.

The butcher came lumbering up the street. He smiled at the sight of Antonio beside his shop door. "Well, if it isn't Antonio."

Inside, Antonio watched as the butcher put on a clean apron and prepared for the day.

"I'm sorry about yesterday," the butcher said as he

tied the strings of the apron across his ample stomach. "Have you found your missing violin?"

"No, sir." Antonio watched Mr. Franco. The butcher reached for a knife from its place near his chopping board and began to sharpen it against the large block of whetstone.

"No, sir," Antonio said again. At the sight of the knife, Antonio had to resist the urge to run from the shop.

The butcher tested the sharpness of the blade against his thumb. "Well, what can I do for you today? Is it sausages or violins this time?"

"Violins." And keeping his eyes away from the knife, Antonio asked his new question. "Mr. Franco, do you remember your aunt ever talking about hearing a magic violin?"

"Hmm. Now that's a different matter." The butcher automatically reached for another knife. "No, never . . . not that I remember."

"Please think hard," Antonio urged. But he was very polite as he watched the butcher move the blade of the knife back and forth.

"I'm trying, Antonio. But . . ." The butcher's mind seemed to drift off. His hands kept sharpening one knife after the other. "The only thing maybe I can think of," the butcher said, shaking his head, ". . . but not my aunt."

"Go ahead, Mr. Franco."

"It was Papa Parducci. One night after I played my fiddle he came to me and said, 'I love the sound of the violin. It makes me think of magic.' I thought he was crazy, but maybe . . ."

"Papa Parducci!" Antonio interrupted. He thanked Mr. Franco and headed for the door. Mr. Franco wasn't so bad, in spite of his size and his loud voice. But, taking one last look at the knife in the butcher's hand, Antonio backed out, just in case.

The candle shop was dark and quiet just as it had been the day before. Antonio called out, "Papa Parducci!"

"Eh? Eh?" The old man's voice came through the curtain from the back of the shop.

"It's Antonio." Antonio wondered if Papa Parducci would remember yesterday's visit.

A minute passed before the old man stuck his head through the curtain. "Well, what are you waiting for?" He motioned to Antonio with his cane. "Come on back here."

Antonio had never been invited behind the curtain before, and he was not prepared for what he saw. From the floor to the ceiling, every inch of the room, except for a spot in the middle, was filled with things—old, dusty, broken things. There were grimy glass bottles, battered copper pots, and tarnished candlestick holders. There were chipped pottery jars, cracked lamps, and lanterns with missing parts. Antonio couldn't begin to list what he saw in the room.

Papa Parducci shuffled about. "So many memories . . . so many memories in my life." He stopped and swept the room with his cane. "These things help me remember."

And Antonio understood for the first time why the old man couldn't always remember. Papa Parducci had lived so long that he had more things in his mind than Antonio could even imagine.

How could he make Papa Parducci remember? Gently he spoke. "Papa Parducci, do you have something in this room that reminds you of your mother?"

The man seemed confused. Antonio began to think it would end like the day before. Then Papa Parducci moved to a cupboard against one wall. He pulled from it a vase decorated with pink and red roses. It was cracked and chipped and very dusty. "This belonged to my mother. She was called Angelina, you know . . . and her mother, too."

Antonio nodded, not saying a word. The old man's eyes, though they filled with tears, seemed alert for the first time.

Carefully, Antonio asked his question: "Papa Parducci, did your mother ever talk about hearing a magic violin?"

Antonio held his breath.

Papa Parducci began to talk. His voice sounded like that of a little child. "Mother said a rhyme to me."

Antonio waited for him to go on, but Papa Parducci stood there looking down at the vase. Antonio whispered, "It is a beautiful vase, Papa Parducci. The rhyme . . . the rhyme . . . can you say the rhyme?"

Hesitantly, Papa Parducci began to speak:
"Magic violin play me a tune.
Stop the rain and stop it soon."

Antonio tried to keep the excitement out of his

voice. "What does it mean, Papa Parducci? What does it mean? What does the violin have to do with rain? And magic?"

But the old man's eyes clouded over again.

Antonio left the shop. As he closed the door, he heard Papa Parducci say, "What do you want? I have candles, lots of candles."

CHAPTER
7

The Monastery

The sun was moving toward its midmorning spot when Antonio came out of the candle shop. He ran for home to tell Luigi the new clue.

With his head down and his mind full of the rhyme, he didn't see the mayor until it was too late.

"Where are you going, boy?" the mayor said.

Antonio looked up at the sun again, checking the time. "I have to get home, Mr. Mayor."

"Just a minute. Don't be in such a rush. Why didn't you come back yesterday and report to me?"

"I'm sorry, Mr. Mayor, but we didn't find the violin ... or anything ... until just now." Antonio regretted the words even before they were out of his mouth.

"Just now? What happened just now?" The mayor pulled Antonio into his shop. Antonio, as quickly as he could, told of his visit to see Mr. Franco and Papa Parducci. He repeated his question and recited the rhyme.

"Slow down, boy. Say that rhyme again. I am the mayor, you know."

Antonio had an idea. What if the mayor knew the meaning of the rhyme? That would make the new clue that much better.

Antonio slowed down and said the rhyme again:
"Magic violin play me a tune,
Stop the rain and stop it soon."

Then, making sure all the words came out right—for he had no time to make a mistake—he said, "Mr. Mayor, because you are the mayor, do you know what the rhyme means? Why would a magic violin stop the rain?"

The mayor's face grew red. He cleared his throat. He looked over at the robe and the red ribbon with the official looking medal at its end where they hung on the rack beside his desk. "I told you the names, didn't I?"

"But the rhyme, Mr. Mayor," Antonio insisted. "Do you know about the rhyme?"

"Well I can't be expected to know everything. I know about births, marriages, and deaths. But violins and magic are not my responsibility. Neither is the weather."

"Oh," Antonio said. For the first time he understood something about the mayor. He wasn't nearly as important as he said he was. He just wanted people to think he was. And Antonio felt sorry for the little man.

The mayor cleared his throat. He looked down at the floor. "You should ask at the monastery. They know everything up there. Ask Brother Bernardo. He keeps the records." And the mayor pushed Antonio from his shop.

Antonio ran home. He told Luigi what had happened. They decided to go to the monastery.

It was the next morning when they started up the hill. It wasn't long before they left the rooftops of the town below. The gray walls of the ancient building lay above at the crest of the hill.

Antonio had never been to the monastery. He was nervous.

His mother had made him wash extra well. She had combed his hair until he thought it would fall out. And all the time she had given him a million instructions on how to act and what to say. She had even wanted him to put on his shoes, but somehow he had escaped that.

Now Antonio walked beside Luigi, glad to be outside in the morning sun with his new friend. "What will you do when we find the violin?"

Luigi looked at Antonio and laughed. "It's good to hear you are so sure we will find the violin, *amico mio.*"

Antonio smiled. He was certain. He repeated his question. "What will you do when we find it?"

Luigi began his list: "I will study it. I'll check the label, of course. I will measure the violin for its length and for the thickness of its wood. Stradivari was very precise about that. I'll tap the wood to make sure it has not lost its resonance and check the varnish to be sure it has not been damaged—that is very important." Luigi paused for a minute as if checking the list. "Oh yes, if the violin needs to be repaired, I'll do that. I always carry my tools."

Antonio thought of the strange assortment on the makeshift table in the shed. His heart jumped a beat. Now he knew.

They walked on in silence.

After a while Antonio asked, "Did you ever repair a Stradivarius violin?"

"I did. The first time I held a great Stradivarius in my hands it changed my life forever."

Antonio nodded. He had not held the violin yet. Still, it was definitely changing his life.

The hill was steeper now. Luigi stopped to catch his breath.

Antonio waited beside him. "After you repair our violin," he asked, "will you put it in the box and take it to Milan?"

"Yes. But first I must play it. I need to know it still has its voice."

The Violin Man started up the hill again. Antonio chased after him. "Play it?" he shouted. "You do that, too?"

Luigi laughed at the look on Antonio's face. "When I was young like you," he explained, "I thought I would be the world's greatest violinist. I practiced very hard." Luigi moved about, playing an imaginary violin.

"But, alas, I did not have the hands for it." He held up his hands. "My music making, while good, was never great. I would have been lucky to have a place in the opera orchestra in Milan. I gave up my dream of playing."

He stopped and looked down at Antonio. "But my passion for violins would not go away. I turned to hunting for them. Which sometimes is almost as good."

With all this flying through Antonio's mind, he ran ahead.

He waited for Luigi at the top of the hill.

Together they gazed out across the valley. Beyond the valley there was another valley, and beyond that another, and another. Straining his eyes, Antonio imagined he could see all of Italy.

A pair of eagles, with feathers the color of tarnished gold, soared over them and swept down into the valley.

"A good omen," the Violin Man whispered as they followed the flight.

They walked the short distance to the entrance of the monastery.

Antonio stood before the enormous weathered door. He felt very small. It took all his courage to reach for the long bell chain that hung to one side. He gave the chain a hard pull. From somewhere far inside there was the clang of a bell. It was followed by silence.

Antonio was about to pull the chain again when the door opened. It gave out a great creak of old age.

A young man stood within, examining the visitors. He wore a long robe. His face was barely visible within the frame of the robe's hood.

"Peace be with you," he said. His voice was hushed and calm.

"And with you," Luigi replied.

Antonio leaned forward to make himself heard. "I'm Antonio, from the town. This is Luigi. We would like to speak to Brother Bernardo." His voice squeaked strangely.

Without a word, the man bowed and closed the door, leaving them to wait outside. When at last he returned, he motioned them to follow him.

Antonio and Luigi obeyed his instructions. They walked single file through the covered walkways and out to a courtyard.

Brother Bernardo sat on a stone bench near a fountain. An open book rested in his lap. His eyes stared into space.

As they approached, Brother Bernardo set aside his book. "Ah, Antonio, it is good to see you. And who is this?"

"This is Luigi, Brother Bernardo. He has come to town searching for something very old and very beautiful." Antonio spoke properly, just as his mother had told him.

"Well, I am old, there is no doubt about that. But I am not very beautiful, so it cannot be me for whom he is looking." Brother Bernardo smiled at them and the smile seemed to light up his whole face.

It was a round face. Its roundness went well with the fringe of graying hair that encircled his head. His round head seemed to sit directly on his round body. In fact, Brother Bernardo was round all over, right down to the round toes that peeked out from the round hem of his robe.

Luigi began to speak. He spoke with such care and dignity that Antonio was sure he had been to a monastery many times before. "Brother Bernardo, I am known as the Violin Man. I travel about the country looking for rare violins."

"Ah yes," Brother Bernardo said, "I have heard of such violins. They are called Stradivarius violins, are they not?"

Antonio couldn't believe it. Brother Bernardo already knew about the violin. It made the telling of the story much faster.

Antonio filled in the facts about their search. He told him about the diary, the mayor's ledgers, Mr. Franco, and Papa Parducci. He told him about the wrong question, the right question, and the rhyme.

He finished with, "And the mayor told us that only the monastery keeps records of things like weather and violins . . . and magic." The last word was barely audible.

Brother Bernardo listened, nodding his head at each step of the way. "Say the rhyme, Antonio."

Antonio recited it just as Papa Parducci had done the day before:

"Magic violin, play me a tune.

Stop the rain, and stop it soon."

Brother Bernardo looked directly at Luigi. His smile was radiant. "Perhaps we do have your violin, Mr. Violin Man. Perhaps we do."

CHAPTER
8

The Story

Brother Bernardo motioned for Antonio and Luigi to be seated. The Violin Man sat on the stone bench beside him, while Antonio settled at his feet.

Doubling his legs up to his chin and hugging himself, Antonio was ready to listen. And the story began.

"Once, long ago, Antonio, something happened in our town that had never happened before. For three years in a row, the rains came in August just when the grapes needed the sun. Because of this, the grapes rotted on the vines. For three autumns there was no harvest. For three winters the people of the town went hungry and cold because they had no money. It was a sad time for everyone."

Antonio nodded. He often heard his father worry about the rains.

Brother Bernardo went on. "During the third winter without rain, a stranger came to the town. He told his story.

"He had been a court musician for a wealthy count who loved violin music. Some years before the count had bought a beautiful violin and hired this musician to play it for him each night."

At the word violin, Antonio smiled up into the round face of Brother Bernardo. The man reached out and patted Antonio on the head as he continued his story.

"Then one year a terrible thing happened. The lands of the count were invaded, and the count knew he would have to fight. One night he sent for the musician and said, 'You must go and take the violin with you. If it stays here, the enemy will most surely destroy it. When peace comes, you will bring the violin back to me so my life can once again be filled with its music.'

"That night, with the violin hidden under his cloak and a few pieces of gold in his purse, the court musician fled. He had not gone far before he looked back. There against the dark night, flames were shooting high into the sky. The musician was sad. He knew he would never again play the violin for the count who had loved it so.

"The man wandered about looking for a place to

live. A place that would be safe. A place where he could play his violin. And it was then he came to our town."

Antonio moved a little closer to Brother Bernardo as the story continued.

"But the people of the town did not want the man. 'There are already enough people in this town to feed,' they said.

"He showed them he had enough gold for one year of food and lodging. And he refused to leave.

"The people would have nothing to do with him. During the day he went about offering help where he could, but they always refused. At night, because he had no friends, he stayed by himself. Alone in his room, he played his violin."

Brother Bernardo studied his round toes for a minute before picking up his story. "After a while, Antonio, the people, hearing sounds of the violin, began to gather outside his dwelling. They were drawn to the music. Night after night they stood listening. As if by magic they forgot their hunger and the cold.

"The next spring the rains came and made the vines grow, and the grapes appeared. When summer arrived the rains stopped, the sun came out, and the grapes grew to be full and ripe.

"That autumn the town was blessed with the best harvest in its memory. Even the oldest people in the town could not remember a time when the grapes had been so many or so sweet.

"That winter, tables were filled with food. Once again there was fuel for the fires. And people began to talk about the man and his violin. 'It was the magic of the violin that stopped the rain,' they said.

"Even the children of the town, as they played their games, told of the magic in their rhymes."

Antonio had been concentrating so hard that he did not notice when the storyteller finished.

"Well, Antonio," Brother Bernardo said, "that is the story of your rhyme."

Antonio sat there not knowing what to make of it all.

Luigi, a brightness in his eyes, leaned toward Brother Bernardo and said quietly, "Do you know the name of this man with the violin?"

Brother Bernardo shook his head at the question. "No. If I ever knew, I have forgotten now." He thought for a minute longer. "He stayed on in the town, married, and had a family. They lived in peace and happiness in the years that followed."

"We need to know the family name," the Violin Man urged once more.

"Let's go into the archives then. If there is a written record, it will be there." Brother Bernardo stood. He folded his hands within his robe and led the way. Antonio and Luigi followed.

Brother Bernardo's love for the archives was plain to see. He motioned around the room. "Here are the written records of all that has ever happened since our monastery was built."

Antonio looked around the room. Along one wall narrow windows reached from the floor to the ceiling, letting in beams of gentle yellow light. All the other walls were covered with shelves and cupboards. And all of these were filled with books and manuscripts.

Brother Bernardo looked around. "Let me see," he said. He pointed to a shelf along the far wall. "Ah yes, it would be about there."

Antonio wondered how, with all these books and manuscripts, anyone could know where anything was.

"Yes, this is it," Brother Bernardo said. He walked to the shelf to pull down a giant book with a thick wooden cover. The book was so heavy that Brother Bernardo nearly toppled from its weight. Antonio reached forward just in time to save him. Together they placed the book on a table.

Brother Bernardo opened the book. He bent close to the pages, working very hard to see in the dim light. He began to scan the writing. The crackle of the paper, brittle with age, echoed through the room as

Brother Bernardo turned page after page.

"No . . . no," he muttered over and over. His fingers moved down one page and then another. His forehead wrinkled with concentration. He looked up once in a while as if surprised to see Luigi and Antonio still standing there.

Just as Antonio was about to give up, Brother Bernardo gave a sigh of relief and said, "Ah yes, here it is."

The man raised his round head that topped his round body and his round toes. He smiled the smile that seemed to light his whole face. He looked at his two visitors and said, "Palermo— that was the man's name—Palermo."

Antonio let out a gasp.

CHAPTER
9

The Oak Chest

Antonio didn't remember thanking Brother Bernardo. He didn't remember walking down the hill. The name Palermo crowded his head, making it difficult for him to concentrate.

When they reached town, Antonio tugged at Luigi's arm. "Come," he said. "We'll find the violin at the Widow Palermo's."

Luigi pulled back. "We'll have to wait until late in the day, Antonio. Midday isn't the time to visit someone."

Antonio had no choice. He had to wait.

The cooling shadows of afternoon were crossing the town as Luigi and Antonio stopped before the old

Palermo house. The house sagged with age in a strange downhill fashion.

Antonio stepped to the door and knocked. A minute later it opened.

The Widow Palermo looked out at them. Even though she was young, she wore the black dress of a widow. Her hair, carefully pulled back in a knot, was still a shiny jet black. Her eyes were bright. A baby slept soundly in her arms. Two children hid in the folds of her skirt.

Widow Palermo glanced first to Antonio and then to Luigi. She waited for them to speak.

"Good afternoon, Widow Palermo," Antonio began. His voice squeaked. He had never been to Widow Palermo's house before.

"This is Luigi. He's my friend," he said. "May we come in and talk to you?"

Without a word, the widow stepped aside and let them pass. The doorway to the ancient house was so low the Violin Man had to duck his head. Inside, the ceiling was not much higher.

The walls were smooth and white. The window at the front of the house was still shuttered against the afternoon heat. It was dark and cool in the room.

The widow motioned for them to sit on a wooden bench. She took her place in a chair facing them. The two children stood behind her, peeking out at Luigi and Antonio.

The widow rocked her baby and waited for Antonio or Luigi to begin. Antonio looked around the room. He shook himself and forced his eyes back to where the widow sat.

"Luigi has come to town looking for something very important," he said.

"I have come in search of a rare violin with a most beautiful sound," Luigi added.

The Widow Palermo sat there without a word.

"It's called a Stradivarius," Antonio explained.

"We have reason to believe it was owned by your family at one time," Luigi said.

Still, the widow sat there.

Antonio tried again. "Brother Bernardo told us a story about a violin and a man named Palermo," he said. "And we wonder if you . . . well, we hope . . ."

Luigi laughed softly. "We hope you have the violin."

The Widow Palermo adjusted the blanket around her baby.

"Sir," she said softly, "I'm a poor widow with three children to raise. My husband died too young. He left no money to take care of me and his children. I have nothing but a sad heart."

"But if you have the violin," Antonio offered, "maybe it will make you happy again. They say it has magic."

Widow Palermo shook her head. "I don't believe in magic, Antonio."

"If you have the violin, I could take it to Milan," Luigi said, "and find someone to buy it. Your share of the money would take care of you for the rest of your life. I'm sure your husband would have wanted that."

"I see," the widow said. She rose and carried her baby to the cradle. She stood there looking down at the sleeping child.

"You have come to the wrong place," she said when she returned to her chair. "I do wish to be happy again. And enough money to care for my children would be more than I could ever dream of."

The widow folded and unfolded her hands twice before she added, "Still, you have come to the wrong place. My husband did not play a violin. He worked in the vineyards."

"Oh, it wouldn't have been your husband, Widow Palermo." Antonio slipped off the bench and moved close to her. "This violin is very old," he confided. "Maybe ten times older than I am."

For the first time, the Widow Palermo smiled. "That is very old, indeed, Antonio," she said.

Luigi searched the widow's eyes. "Is it possible your husband's father or grandfather owned such a violin?" he asked. "Please," he added, "it is important that you remember. Could the violin be somewhere in this house?"

The widow studied both Antonio and Luigi. "I am sure my husband would have told me if he owned such a precious thing."

She shook her head. "No, I'm sorry, I cannot help you."

The widow stood up. "Good day," she said.

Antonio fell back against the bench. It's over, he thought. He slumped there, waiting for Luigi to say the farewells.

But the Violin Man didn't move. "Do you have an attic?" he asked.

"Yes." The widow glanced upward. "But I don't go

up there anymore. There are too many memories. I have cried enough."

"Sometimes memories can be music to your soul," Luigi said gently.

"Will you take us to the attic?" Antonio asked.

The Widow Palermo shook her head. "No, I think not."

"Please," Antonio pleaded. He was by her side now. "The violin might be up there."

The widow's mouth formed a sad little smile. She thought for a minute. "Only for you, Antonio."

Widow Palermo lit a lantern and led the way to the back of the house, where a steep stairway disappeared into the ceiling.

Lifting the lantern high, she climbed the stairs. Her children followed, holding on to her skirt. Antonio came next. Last came Luigi.

At the top of the stairs, the widow pushed at a large trap door. It fell back with a crash. Cautiously, she entered the darkness of the attic. One by one, the children, Antonio, and Luigi followed.

They stood in a tight circle within the light of the lantern. A mouse scampered by and out of sight. A musty smell surrounded them. Old clothes hung about on pegs like unworldly guests.

Antonio looked back to be sure he knew the way out. He moved a little closer to Luigi.

Luigi didn't seem to mind the darkness. He left the light and peered into boxes that were piled everywhere. Here and there he moved a piece of leftover furniture to look behind. Soon the whole attic was filled with dust.

Still, he did not find the violin.

Finally Luigi pulled a large box from one corner of the attic. Behind the box was a chest made of oak.

"There!" Luigi pointed in triumph. "Don't you think that would be a fine hiding place for a violin?"

Widow Palermo walked over for a better view. She moved the lantern over the chest. She blew at the dust that covered the lid. "From the looks of it," she said, "this chest has been here for a long time."

Antonio followed her. "Open it," he urged.

The widow pulled back. "I'm not sure I should."

"You'll never know what joy might be inside if you don't try," Luigi said.

"Or what sadness," the widow replied. Then she looked into Antonio's eyes. "Very well," she sighed.

She handed the lantern to Luigi and knelt before the chest. Her children moved to stand beside her. Antonio stood as close as he dared.

She pushed at the lid. It didn't open. She pushed again. And again. Then she pushed once more. And with a sharp crack the lid swung back.

They all leaned forward at once. The chest was full!

Carefully, the widow began to take things out.

There were beautiful linens turned ivory with age. There was a silver candlestick holder covered with years of tarnish. There were six deep red crystal tumblers. They sparkled in the light of the lantern.

"Such beautiful things," the widow said. "I never imagined they were here." She looked at her children. "Perhaps they belonged to your grandmother," she said.

The widow pulled out an ancient wedding dress

and a pressed bouquet of flowers. "Here was someone's joyful memory." Her eyes glistened. "How well I remember my own wedding day."

She took out baby clothes. A mother had folded them away with special care. The widow held them to her cheek. There were happy tears in her eyes.

After a few minutes the chest was empty— except for a package at the bottom. Widow Palermo stared down at it.

Luigi held the lantern closer. "Could this be our treasure?" he wondered aloud. Still, he did not reach out for it.

Only Antonio seemed able to move. He bent over and pulled the bundle from the chest.

The Widow Palermo began to cry. She stood up and clung to her children.

Luigi spoke in a hushed voice. "Open it, Antonio."

Antonio removed the string that held the wrapping tightly in place. He removed the layers of cloth, one at a time, until only one layer was left. Slowly he pulled it away.

There in his hands was a violin, glowing in the light of the lantern like an amber jewel.

Luigi reached across and slowly rubbed his hand over its smooth finish.

The Widow Palermo ran a timid finger around the carving of the scroll.

From somewhere Antonio found just enough voice to ask, "Is it a Stradivarius?"

CHAPTER
10

And Then...

Is it a Stradivarius?" Antonio asked for what seemed the hundredth time since the violin had been found. The violin lay on the makeshift table, its satin finish catching the soft morning light from the shed's tiny window. Antonio sat with his elbows on the table, his chin cupped in his hands, looking down at the violin.

Luigi sat beside him. His hands caressed the grain of the wood for what seemed the thousandth time. "I'm not sure, Antonio. The violin is old, that I know. But a Stradivarius . . ." And Luigi's voice trailed away. Antonio gave a disgusted grunt. He had waited all night for Luigi to decide.

"What does the label say?" he insisted.

"It's too faint to tell." Luigi picked up the violin and once again tried to see inside.

"Then we'll never know."

"Don't give up, Antonio." Luigi pointed to a place on the side of the violin where the seams of the wood were coming apart. "See—it needs repair. I'll just take off the top. We can take a better look inside."

Antonio watched as Luigi looked over the objects on the table and chose a knife with a long narrow blade. As if cutting open a melon, he inserted the knife between the top and the rib of the violin. Being very cautious now, he separated the top from the rest of the violin and placed it to one side.

Antonio ducked his head in close and tried to read the label, but he couldn't make it out.

"Maybe this will help." Luigi picked up the magnifying glass from the table. He held it over the violin and adjusted it back and forth until he found a focus.

Luigi studied the label. The Violin Man let out an occasional "ah" and then an occasional "hmm" which didn't tell Antonio a single thing.

Finally Luigi nodded. "Take a look, Antonio."

Antonio took Luigi's place above the magnifying glass. He worked to make his eyes focus. Now the label was easy to see.

Slowly he read, *"Anton Stradivarius . . . Cremonensis . . . 1736."* His head popped up to look at Luigi.

Luigi returned his smile. "Antonio Stradivari always wrote his labels in Latin."

Antonio took another look. This time when his

head came up from the magnifying glass he demanded the answer to his question: "Is it a Stradivarius?"

There was a new sparkle in the Violin Man's eyes.

"Then it *is* a Stradivarius violin," Antonio said.

"I'm beginning to think so, still . . ."

"Still?" Antonio insisted.

"Still, we should make sure."

"When will we know?" Antonio let out a big sigh.

Luigi laughed. "It takes patience, Antonio."

But Antonio couldn't wait. "Is it all right if I tell everyone we think we've found a Stradivarius?"

"Yes, but . . ."

Antonio shot from the shed and raced to tell the news.

Antonio reported all the details to the mayor. He made sure the mayor knew it was an official report.

"Of course, Antonio. With my help, you couldn't fail," the mayor replied.

As Antonio moved on he thought: The mayor didn't call me boy—not once.

Then he stopped at the butcher shop, opened the door, and yelled. "Hooray, Mr. Franco! We found the violin!"

"Good for you, Antonio," the butcher yelled back. "I knew you could do it." Mr. Franco and his knives didn't bother Antonio anymore.

Antonio woke Papa Parducci from his nap. "Papa Parducci, your magic violin—it has been found."

Antonio was surprised when the old man answered, "Why it's Antonio. That's good news, son. You make me a happy man."

As Antonio left the shop, Papa Parducci sat wide awake in his chair. He smiled and nodded in rhythm, as if the magic violin were echoing through his head. Antonio knocked on the Widow Palermo's door. "We're almost sure about the violin. You'll be rich!"

"Dear Antonio, how can I thank you?" the widow answered.

Antonio stopped people in the street who didn't even know about the violin.

"Good for you," and "*deo gracias*," they called after him.

He found some of his friends playing tag. When he told them about the violin, he hoped they noticed he wasn't the least bit ordinary anymore.

The rest of that day Antonio stayed by Luigi's side while the Violin Man worked on the violin. Antonio watched Luigi measure its length to within a sixteenth of an inch. "That's right for a Stradivarius," the Violin Man said.

Antonio was there when Luigi used his strange pair of pliers that looked like the ones used by the barber to pull teeth. Calipers, he called them. "To measure the thickness of the wood," he explained. "Just to make sure."

Antonio liked it when Luigi tested the violin for its resonance. It made a wonderful sound as he flicked his finger against the wood. Luigi seemed pleased with what he heard.

Luigi looked at the varnish through the magnifying glass and smiled. "Sometimes the varnish is ruined. But this has grown better with age."

As Luigi worked, he and Antonio talked about all

sorts of things. Antonio asked questions; Luigi tried to find answers.

At last Antonio asked Luigi the one question he had wanted to ask ever since the violin had been found. "The violin—do you think it is magic?"

"I don't know, Antonio," Luigi answered truthfully.

"Do you think that it kept the townspeople from being cold and hungry, like Brother Bernardo said?"

"I don't know," Luigi repeated. He looked up from his work long enough to add, "But music can do amazing things. It can make you forget your worries. So if that is what this violin did, then maybe it is magic."

Antonio was quiet for a long time after that.

When everything was cleaned and checked, Luigi heated his pot of glue over the little stove. He applied the glue around the edge of the front of the violin and put it back where it belonged.

He took the wooden clamps and placed them around the edge of the violin. He tightened them until the top was held firmly in place.

Luigi straightened up from his work. "It's done," he said with a relieved stretch of his back. "Now we must wait for the glue to dry, and then . . ."

"Then we'll know for sure?"

"Then I will replace the sound post." Luigi showed Antonio how he would cut a piece from the small round stick of doweling to make the sound post. And how, using the strange metal hook as a fishing pole, he would drop the sound post into the violin and force it upright between the front and back of the violin until it was in its place between the sound holes.

"And then?" Antonio couldn't believe anything else could be done to the violin.

"And then I will have to make a bridge to support the strings." Luigi held up a thin slab of wood that would become the bridge. "And then I'll put on the strings." He pointed to the strings Antonio hadn't noticed before.

"And then?" Antonio was beginning to believe the "and thens" would never stop.

Luigi smiled. "And then, Antonio, *amico mio*, it will be time for us to hear if our violin still has its beautiful voice."

CHAPTER
11

The Day

Antonio was up before anyone else in the house. Today was the day. The violin was ready to be played.

Before long the people of the town began to gather in front of Antonio's house.

Antonio stood watching them arrive. They all greeted him. He felt very special.

The mayor came, dressed in his black robe and red ribbon with a medal at the end. He reminded anyone who would listen that as the mayor he had played a very important part in finding the violin.

Mr. Franco came up the street from his shop, puffing from the steepness of the climb. When he caught his breath, he laughed a lot and told how he had given Antonio his clue.

Even Papa Parducci came, using his cane to help him up the hill. He kept reciting his rhyme over and over.

The Widow Palermo, when she finally appeared, stood apart from the others. She kept her children pressed to her as if she did not dare believe what was happening.

Brother Bernardo did not appear, but somehow, when a warm breeze floated down from the top of the hill, Antonio knew he was thinking of the violin, nevertheless.

Antonio's mother stood beside him, her arm around his shoulder. His brothers and sisters lined up behind them. Antonio's father had stayed in from the fields and was there to watch.

At the appointed time, Luigi arrived from the shed carrying the violin in one hand and a bow in the other. He took his place beneath the tree. He smiled at the people as they gathered close.

Luigi had a special look for Antonio—a look that seemed to say: "Well, Antonio, we will soon know."

Antonio nodded his answer: "It will have its special voice, Violin Man. I just know it will."

Luigi tucked the violin under his chin. He poised the bow just above the strings. The crowd hushed. Time seemed to stop.

Just when Antonio was sure he couldn't wait a minute longer, Luigi began to play. It was a sad melody that soared to the top of the violin and back down again. It reminded Antonio of the golden

eagles in flight. A good omen, he thought.

Suddenly the music changed. It was as if the violin wanted to dance. Luigi laughed as he followed along. His bow bounced about and his fingers flew over the strings.

Antonio grinned. His feet moved to the rhythm of the melody. His mother looked down at him and moved her head in time to the music. Even his father smiled.

The mayor tugged at his medal. Mr. Franco threw

his head back and laughed out loud from pure joy. Papa Parducci found the beat with his cane. The Widow Palermo stood by, smiling and crying at the same time. And a warm breeze floated down from the top of the hill.

Too soon, the music was over. Luigi put the violin down and looked at it. He turned it over and over. The crowd stood still. They waited. Antonio waited, too. Slowly the Violin Man raised his head, a smile spreading across his face. "We found our Stradivarius violin, Antonio. We truly did!"

Antonio let out a shout. The crowd roared.

The mayor cleared his throat but he did not speak. Mr. Franco covered his face with his hands so no one could see the large tear that fell down his cheek. Papa Parducci found a seat and sat down to rest. "It's magic," he mumbled to himself. The Widow Palermo held her children close to her. She whispered a prayer of thanks. And a warm breeze floated down from the top of the hill.

Soon, after an unusual amount of hugging and laughing, the people of the town went down the hill and on to whatever they had to do.

Antonio and Luigi stood beneath the tree. They did not talk. No words were needed for what they were feeling.

Back in the shed, Luigi prepared to leave. With Antonio's help, he opened the box with its blue velvet lining and placed the violin inside.

Antonio worked not to cry. But somehow one tear escaped and fell on the box just as the lid closed.

"Where . . . where will you stay tonight?" he asked.

"In the city just beyond the hills at the end of the valley."

"What will you do then?"

"I'll catch a train . . . tomorrow . . . to Milan."

"A train?"

"Yes, a train," Luigi affirmed.

Antonio was quiet.

Then he said, "What will you do in Milan?"

"I'll go to a dealer of instruments, and he will find someone to buy our violin."

"And then what will you do?"

"Oh, I will start all over—looking for another Stradivarius."

"Will I ever see you again?" Antonio could hardly get the words out.

"I think so. I'll bring back the Widow Palermo's share of the money for the violin. I'll see you then."

"Oh."

"But . . ." Luigi stopped his packing. He stared down at the magnifying glass he had been about to place in his pack, not really seeming to see it. "But . . . just maybe, if your parents would let you, you could go with me to take the violin." Luigi looked straight at Antonio. "Would you like that?"

Antonio's eyes grew wider than they had ever been in his whole life. "Go with you! Do you mean it?"

"I don't see why not. You found the violin, didn't you? I think you should see who finally plays it."

"Would we go on a train?"

"Yes, of course. Would you like that?" Luigi laughed, already knowing the answer to that question. "And you can come back with me when I bring the money for the Widow Palermo."

Antonio ran, shouting, into the house to ask his mother and father if he could go with the Violin Man.

His mother and father talked together for a long time, and then they talked even longer with the Violin Man.

Antonio stood by. His fingers were crossed; his eyes were shut. He was wishing as hard as he could. If the violin is magic, let it work now, he thought.

Soon the answer came.

"Yes, Antonio," his mother said. She shed a tear and added, "We will miss you."

"Yes, Antonio," his father said. He frowned and added, "I hope you will settle down when you come home."

They both agreed they trusted Luigi. They knew Antonio would be safe.

It was midmorning when Luigi lifted his heavy pack to his back.

Antonio had a pack, too. In it his mother had put a change of clothes and some food. "Just in case you get hungry," she said. She insisted on his taking a comb and soap, too, although he couldn't see why. She even made him tuck his shoes into the bottom of his pack, saying he definitely couldn't go to the big city without shoes.

When the time came for them to leave, Luigi adjusted his pack and tested its balance. Then he helped Antonio with his. When Antonio's pack was secure, Luigi tied the box to the top of it. "There, you can carry the violin. It's not too heavy for you, is it?''

Antonio's pride at carrying the violin in its box with the blue velvet lining made it feel like a feather on his back.

They said good-bye to Antonio's mother and father. They said good-bye to his brothers and sisters.

And they started down through the town with its houses pressed against the narrow street. Antonio walked with his head held high to let everyone know that now he was a traveling man.

The whole town followed them. First there was the mayor, who reminded Luigi that he was indeed the mayor. Then there was Mr. Franco, who had closed his shop just specially to come. Then there was the Widow Palermo and her children. And finally there was Papa Parducci. Brother Bernardo was not there, but somehow Antonio knew he was watching from the top of the hill.

Everyone stood at the edge of town and waved to Antonio and Luigi.

When Antonio reached the first bend in the road, he turned to look back. He would miss his family. He would miss his town and his friends.

With a last look, he turned, adjusted his pack, and fell into step with Luigi.

Together Antonio and the Violin Man made their way to the bottom of the hill. They turned north, following the road that led to the city just beyond the hills. They walked steadily without once stopping to rest. They walked all through the morning and on into the afternoon. They walked up the valley until they disappeared from sight.